CHLOE, WHERE ARE YOU?

Written by Lynn Marie Lusch

Edited by Randi Marie Gause

Lynn Marie Lusch

CONTENTS

DAY OFF FROM SCHOOL

Yippee! I get the whole day off from school today! It's a special Teacher's Meeting Day, so all the students have the day off.

My name is Lindsey Marie Robbins, I'm seven years old and in the second grade at Bay View Elementary School in Bay View, California. Even though I really like school, today is going to be a lot of fun!

I live in a big, white, two-story house with my mom and dad, big sister Lacey, and my little sister Lauren. I also have a six month old puppy named Chloe. She has long black hair, a white chin, and a white mark on her chest. Her eyes are so dark brown that you almost can't see them because they blend with the fur on her face!

Today I'm going over to my best friend's house. Her name is Melissa and her mom said she can redecorate her bedroom, and I get to help! Melissa likes to take pictures, mostly of butterflies and birds when she can sneak up on them. She takes pictures of neighborhood cats and dogs, too. She took a lot of Chloe when we adopted her.

Melissa got a new printer for her birthday, so her mom said she can print some of her pictures and pin them up on her bedroom walls. I get to help her pick out the best ones. This is going to be fun, and a hard job. Melissa has a lot of pictures!

I decided to wear my white T-shirt with butterflies on it and blue shorts. I have brown eyes and long brown hair, all the way to my waist! I picked out a multi colored hair band that matches all the butterflies on my shirt.

Lacey was getting ready to ride her bike over to the school and watch the boys in her class play a soccer game. Lacey is eleven years old and in the sixth grade. She has long brown hair too, and braces on her teeth. She had on her red school T shirt with a soccer ball on it, and black shorts. She's meeting her best friend, Jamie, at the game. The whole class will be there, and she's excited! She loves to watch soccer games and cheer for her class.

ONE MUDDY PUPPY

Lacey and I went running down the stairs together and out the back door to tell Dad we're leaving. Dad took the day off of work to get some chores done in the yard. He was mostly planting rose bushes that my mom has been wanting for a long time. They are going to line the fence in the back yard. Dad has bags of fresh dirt and six rose bushes ready to plant. They are so pretty, Mom picked out all different colors- red, pink, peach, yellow, white and orange. Mom is at her yoga class now and Dad wants to have them planted to surprise her when she gets home.

Lauren is running around the back yard with Chloe, pretending to be a dog, too. She is always pretending to be something. She's three years old and has a very good imagination. Lauren is in a pre-school class at our church. Her teacher's name is Miss Phyllis, and Lauren loves to go to school. She has learned a lot of songs and likes to sing all the time, even if she can't remember all of the words.

Lauren is on her hands and knees imitating Chloe. She is even digging in the piles of dirt like Chloe, and they are both a mess! Lauren is covered in dirt, it's even in her hair! Chloe is filthy! You can't even tell she has a white chin!

Lacey and I stood there staring at the mess.

"We were coming to tell you that we're going now," Lacey said to Dad hesitantly.

"I don't think so girls, I need your help. Look at these two!" Dad said. "I can't let either one of them in the house, they'll get dirt everywhere. You two take Chloe and give her a bath, I have to give one to Lauren before your mom gets home. And I wanted to get these bushes planted before the storm comes this afternoon and it starts to rain."

"But Dad!" pleaded Lacey. "I have to go to the soccer game! This is important! I'm meeting everyone there and it's going to start in a few minutes. I'll miss most of the game if I have to give Chloe a bath. Can't Lindsey just do it?"

"But Melissa is waiting for me," I said. "We have the whole day planned. Lacey can do a better job than me and do it faster!" I was starting to whine.

"Ok girls, you both have your day planned, and so do I," Dad said as he was holding a squirming, giggling Lauren. "I can't bathe Lauren and the dog, and besides, Chloe is both your responsibilities, that was the agreement when we adopted her. So you both will give her a bath, then you can go on with your plans."

"Oh Dad no, I'll give her a bath after the soccer game!" Bargained Lacey.

"Lacey, you and Lindsey will give her a bath now. I can't let her in the house, look at how dirty she is! And we can't leave her in the backyard all day, she's too mischievous and has to be watched constantly. She's a pup. Your pup. You can go when you're done."

We knew there was nothing else we could say to change Dad's mind. He was right. Lacey and I begged Mom and Dad to let us adopt Chloe from the shelter, and we promised to bathe her and take care of her. So our fun would have to wait.

"Ahggg" Lacey grumbled. She took out her phone and texted Jamie.

WILL BE LATE. DOG IN TROUBLE. BE THERE AS SOON AS I CAN.

"Let's go Linds. Come on Chloe." She picked the puppy up with her two hands and with her arms stretched straight out. Chloe was so dirty she didn't want to get her clothes messed up.

5

THE BATH

We give Chloe a bath in the big tub in the laundry room. CHLOE HATES BATHS. She constantly tries to climb out, hates to get her face wet, doesn't let us put shampoo on her, and when we finally do and get her all bubbled up she won't let us rinse her. She's always trying to shake her body to get the water off of her. It's a big, messy job, that's why Lacey and I do it together.

"Chloe sit still," Lacey was saying very sternly to Chloe. Lacey was not happy at all about missing the soccer game. Chloe didn't seem to care, she just wanted out of the tub and was doing everything she could to escape from her bath.

Finally, after what seemed like hours, we got her clean. We had about six towels all over the place and were taking turns grabbing Chloe to wipe her and all her hair! What a mess! But Chloe was clean.

We picked her up and carried her outside so she could go potty.

"I'm running up to my room to change my shirt," Lacey said. I looked at the one she was wearing and it was covered with paw prints.

I was watching Chloe run in the grass, smelling anything she could find, when I heard the phone ring. I ran in the kitchen to answer it and it was Melissa.

"Where are you?" Melissa asked. "I thought you were coming over to help me pick out pictures?"

I told her what happened with Chloe and Lauren and said I was done. I was getting ready to jump on my bike and ride down the street to her house.

SHE'S GONE

I went back outside to get Chloe and bring her in the house. I stood there looking all over the yard.

"Chlo! Come on Chloe let's go!" I called.

No Chloe.

"Chloe come on, where are you? Let's go!"

No puppy anywhere.

Lacey came out the back door. She was wearing a different red T-shirt.

"Ok I'm going."

"Lace, I can't find Chloe."

"What do you mean you can't find Chloe?" Lacey asked.

"I ran in the kitchen to answer the phone, and when I came out, she's just not here!"

"She's got to be here," said Lacey, "where else would she be? She can't exactly open the gate." Lacey said sarcastically.

I was running all over the yard looking behind bushes, anywhere a little puppy could hide. Lacey walked into the middle of the yard and started whistling.

"Chloe come on girl, let's go, want a cookie?"

Chloe always comes to you when you call her and promise to give her a treat. We call them cookies.

But No Chloe.

"What's going on girls?" Dad asked, holding a clean Lauren.

"We let Chloe out here to go potty after her bath, and she disappeared," I told him. I was starting to get scared.

"How can she disappear, is the gate closed?" he asked.

"Yeah, that was the first place I looked," I said.

Dad started walking around the yard.

"Oh no," he said.

"What?" Lacey and I said at the same time.

"Look," Dad said, pointing to a pile of dirt. Dad had dug a big hole to plant one of the rose bushes, and the hole went right under the chain-link fence. You could see that the pile of dirt was scrambled.

"Chloe must have started digging again and climbed right under the fence. We need to go find her."

CHLOE, WHERE ARE YOU?

Just then Mom came home from her yoga class.

"What's going on?" she asked when she saw all of our scared faces.

Dad told her what happened.

"Oh boy," Mom said, "let's start looking, she couldn't have gone far."

I thought that too, but when Lacey and I take her for a walk she goes everywhere, or tries to. She pulls on her leash and wants to smell everything, go under everything, go everywhere. She is just a nosey dog!

"Ok," Dad said. "Let's split up. First, let's go where Chloe is familiar, where you two take her on walks."

"Well, we go two different ways." Lacey said.

"Ok, you and I will go one way, and your mom, Lindsey and Lauren will go the other."

We had a plan.

So Dad and Lacey started off down the street, I could hear Dad whistling and Lacey calling Chloe's name. Mom put Lauren in the wagon, which would be faster than Mom carrying her or Lauren trying to keep up with us walking, and we went up the street.

We asked anyone we passed if they saw a little dog, no one saw her.

"Chloe! Come on Chloe!" Mom was calling.

"Chloe, come on let's go home Chloe!" I was calling.

"CHLOE WHERE ARE YOU?" Lauren yelled from the wagon. Boy she can be loud for three years old. Whatever works!

Mom was pulling the wagon as she was looking around. I was running up to bushes, even porches to see if she was hiding.

We couldn't find her. All of a sudden we heard thunder.

"Oh no," Mom said. "We can't stay out much longer, this isn't safe."

"But we can't leave Chloe out in a storm!" I pleaded. I was now officially scared and worried.

"But we can't keep looking for her this way," Mom said. "Let's go home and get the car."

We turned around and went back home, and Dad and Lacey got there at the same time. Empty handed. They didn't find Chloe either.

"I'm going to get the car and go ride around," Dad said.

"I'm coming, too," Lacey and I said at the same time.

"And I will go and send out an alert that there is a missing puppy," Mom said. "I'll get on the computer and send the alert through the company that made the microchip we had the veterinarian put under Chloe's skin at her last appointment."

I forgot about the microchip. It's exactly for this purpose! When we took Chloe to the veterinarian's for her last check up, they asked us if we wanted to microchip her. They put this little tiny computer chip under her skin in her back between her shoulder blades. They showed us one, and it's about as big as a grain of rice. They have a special tool that puts it under her skin. I think it pinched Chloe when they did it, but she was wagging her tail a minute later. It's a tracking device, and when someone waves a special scanner over the spot where they put the microchip, they can read the dog or cat's special number on the scanner, then look it up on the computer and get all of the animal's information.

When we got home from the veterinarian's office that day, Mom signed Chloe up on the company's website. She put in our name, Chloe's name and matching number, what she looks like, Mom's cell phone number, and where we live. If the dog is missing, you put out an alert and everyone that lives near you and is signed up for the same program gets an email or text message telling them that there is a missing dog or cat.

So Mom got on the computer and Lauren stayed home with her. Lacey got in the front seat of the car with Dad and I got in the back. We all had our windows rolled down and Dad drove real slow around the neighborhood. We all took turns calling out Chloe's name.

Lacey's phone jingled because she got a text message. It was from Jamie asking where she was.

CHLOE IS MISSING. GOT OUT THE BACK YARD. WE'RE LOOKING FOR HER, Lacey texted.

Then it started to rain.

"Please don't stop!" Lacey and I begged Dad. We both now started to cry.

"I'm not stopping," Dad said. He really looked worried.

But the rain came down harder. We couldn't even see out of the windshield, and couldn't keep the windows rolled down.

"Let's go back home and see if your mom has had any luck. I promise as soon as the rain stops we'll come back out."

We knew he was right, but we still were crying.

HELP ARRIVES

Dad pulled in the garage and we ran in the house. Mom looked at us, and we could see she was hoping we had good news.

"I posted the alert," Mom said hopefully.

"That's good," Dad said trying to sound confident. "And when the rain lightens up we'll go out again."

Lacey, Lauren and I went to the window and just stared out watching the rain.

Soon the rain seemed to be getting lighter and lighter, and it finally stopped.

Then there was a knock at the door. Dad answered it and it was Andrea and Melissa. Andrea lives in my neighborhood and is in my second grade class, too. They were dressed in their bright pink raincoats and boots. Melissa was holding a plastic bag.

"My mom got an email alert that Chloe is missing!" Andrea said, she sounded very worried.

Her cat had a microchip in him so her Mom got the alert messages.

"I printed up some posters of Chloe with her picture on it," Melissa said. There must have been one hundred! "I put her name on it, your name on it, and your mom's cell phone number. Me and Andrea are going to go pass them out to anyone we see."

Then Jamie came to the door. She was wearing her red school T-shirt and had her dad's big golf umbrella.

"Find the pup yet?" asked Jamie.

"No," said Lacey trembling. "We're getting ready to go back out in the car."

"Didn't she have on that bright pink collar that you ordered for her? The one with her name on it and your mom's cell phone number?" asked Jamie.

"We didn't put it back on her yet," explained Lacey. "We just got done giving her a bath, so she doesn't have any collar on."

"Ok," said Jamie, "I'll help these two pass out posters all over." She was looking at Melissa and Andrea.

Just then Mr. Coleman was on our front porch. He's our next door neighbor.

"Missing a pup?" He asked. Mrs. Coleman came up right behind him.

"I got an alert from the microchip company," she said.

Mrs. Coleman was holding her Yorkie named Wally. He's a pretty golden brown color. He was wearing a blue raincoat. Mrs. Coleman takes him everywhere. She even has a purse with netting on it so she can put him in it and take him into stores with her. Wally is micro-chipped, too. Chloe and Wally run along the chain link fence that separates our yards and bark at each other. Lauren says they're best friends and they're talking.

"Hey I'll take some of those posters," Mr. Coleman said to Melissa. "I'm going to the hardware store and I'll put it up on their bulletin board. I'll stop in the grocery store next to it and put one there too."

Wally in his blue raincoat.

"I'll take some and go to the park," said Mrs. Coleman. "I'll put some there and hand them to anyone I see."

They both took a handful of posters from Melissa and left.

"Ok Pee Wee Squad," Jamie said to Melissa and

Andrea. "Let's go find us a missing puppy." And they left.

We were getting ready to leave and there was another knock on the door. Dad opened it and there stood Daniel and Luke, from Lacey's sixth grade class, and Luke's dog Radar. Daniel and Luke were still wearing their soccer uniforms.

"Hi Mr. Robbins, did you find your dog?" he asked.

"No not yet," Dad answered.

"Well Radar is the best at finding anyone missing," Luke said proudly.

Radar was so big compared to Chloe. She was black and had gold marks on her face and chest. She would seem scary, but she was so friendly! Radar was always wagging her tail and when she licked your face she licked your whole face because her tongue was so long! She was wearing her light pink collar with puppy paws on it, and she looked like she was smiling.

But Luke was right, last summer our neighbor's kitten was missing, and Radar found her under a porch. Radar saved the day and helped find a missing kitten.

"I'll try about anything," Dad said looking at the two boys and the big dog wagging her tail.

Radar

"Can Radar have something of Chloe's to smell?" Luke asked Dad. "So she can get her scent," he said confidently.

"Here's her brush," Lacey said handing it to Luke.

Luke took the brush and put it under Radar's nose.

"Here girl, smell this, now go find Chloe!"

Radar sniffed the brush really hard, and then went walking through the house. She was zig zagging all over with her nose on the carpet, then went to the back door.

"She got out of the yard through a hole under the fence," Lacey told Luke and Daniel, and Radar.

Lacey opened the back door to let Radar and everyone out .

Radar went all over the back yard smelling the grass, then went right over to the hole. She started digging at it.

Dad said, "She may be on to something, here take her through the gate."

So Luke took her through the gate to the other side of the fence where the hole was. Radar picked up the scent and went all over the sidewalk and was going fast! Dad, Luke, Daniel, Lacey and I were running to keep up with her!

Radar went all over the sidewalk, up in a yard, under a bush, and through another yard. She never picked her head up, she just kept sniffing. Down the street, across the street, I started to get worried. I looked at Lacey and I knew she was thinking the same thing. We never took Chloe for a walk this way. Chloe didn't know where she was going, she was just exploring. How were we going to find her!

Radar was still going, still sniffing. We were finally about three blocks away and Radar crossed the street. Luke was running after her. We were on Maple Street. We never walked Chloe this way. Radar went up to a community mailbox and went crazy smelling underneath it. She kept circling the mailbox with her tail wagging. Then she backed up and looked at Luke.

"What is it Radar? Where's Chloe?" he asked

Radar grunted and sat down. She was still looking under the mailbox, still wagging her tail.

"OK," Dad said, "what do you think this means?" he asked looking at Luke.

"Ummm, I really don't know?" Luke said. He looked confused.

"When Radar sits down it usually means she thinks her job is done. But there is nothing here. There's no way Chloe could be in the mailbox. Why does Radar keep smelling under it?" He wondered out loud.

"Come on Radar, find Chloe," Luke said pulling Radar away from the mailbox. He walked a few feet and Radar turned around, went back to the mailbox and smelled under it. She sat down again and grunted.

Then it started to rain.

"Ok boys, I think we're done here. Thanks a lot for trying, thank you Radar," he said to the dog and patted her head. Radar wagged her tail.

"Sorry Lacey," Luke said. He was so disappointed, he really wanted to help.

"That's ok," Lacey said. "Thanks for trying."

Luke put a leash on Radar and he and Daniel started walking away. Dad, Lacey and I started walking back home as the rain started coming down harder.

LAUREN'S IDEA

The storm was scary. It was raining and thundering, and then our power went out. The whole house was dark. Mom got out the candles and started putting them around the house, and Dad got out all of our flashlights.

We all looked at each other. There wasn't anything we could do.

"Lauren, let's go put your pajamas on," Mom said as she took Lauren by the hand and guided her upstairs with a flashlight.

"I can't sleep," Lacey said to me.

"Me either," I answered.

"Well I think it's time for a really good, long bedtime story," Dad said. "Come on, let's go up to Lauren's room."

We went upstairs with our flashlights and went into Lauren's bedroom. Lauren came skipping out of the bathroom in her bright yellow pajamas with fairies on them. The way she was skipping made her look like a fairy.

"When you're happy and you know it clap your hands!" Clap clap. She was singing. Lacey and I looked at each other as if she were crazy.

"Miss Phyllis said if you're sad or scared, sing out loud and it makes you feel better," Lauren said confidently.

"Sounds like a great idea!" Mom said looking at us and trying to smile.

"If you're happy and you know it then your hands are gonna show it if you're happy and you know it clap your hands!" Clap clap.

Dad and Mom clapped, Lacey and I moaned and plopped on Lauren's bed.

"OK story time," Dad said.

Lacey was rolling her eyes at me. The last thing we wanted to do was hear a story.

Lauren grabbed her stuffed white rabbit and climbed up on her bed in between me and Lacey.

"Oh I almost forgot, good night Chloe!" and Lauren leaned over and pet an imaginary dog.

Now Lacey was seriously looking at her like she's weird.

"Miss Phyllis says pretending is good too when you feel sad, it helps happy things happen faster!"

Mom leaned over to the same pretend spot and pet the same imaginary dog.

"Good night Chloe," Mom said, "we'll see you tomorrow."

Dad leaned over and did the same thing, then gave me and Lacey a firm look.

"Whatever," Lacey mumbled under her breath. She and I pet the same imaginary dog.

"And you know what else Miss Phyllis says to do if you're sad?" Lauren asked excitedly.

"Now what?" Lacey was rubbing her forehead with her hand as if she had a headache.

"Miss Phyllis said to say one thing that you are really happy for, and you'll get more things that make you happy! I'm happy I have Miss Phyllis as a teacher!"

Then she looked at Mom.

"Umm ok," Mom said. I could tell she didn't expect this. She thought a minute then said, "I'm happy I finally touched my toes in yoga class this morning."

Then she looked at Lacey.

"Well I'm glad the boys won their soccer game, even if I missed it."

My turn. "I'm happy I still get to help Melissa decorate her bedroom next weekend."

We looked at Dad. "I'm happy we have so many people helping us look for Chloe, and we didn't even ask any of them! They all knew we needed help and just did it on their own." He looked pleased.

Lauren was smiling. "Cinderella!" She said happily to Dad.

"Cinderella it is." Dad said and took that book off of Lauren's bookshelf and sat down on the floor. Mom sat next to him holding the flashlight on the pages so he could read.

I usually like to hear Dad read stories, he uses

different voices and makes them sound real. But I didn't feel like it tonight. I lay there listening to the rain outside and was hoping Chloe was safe and warm. I decided to close my eyes for a little while and just listen to the storm.

THE PHONE CALL

I was punched in the stomach.

I opened my eyes and looked around. I was still lying in Lauren's bed but it was morning, and I wasn't punched in the stomach, I was kicked. I looked down and Lauren's foot was on my stomach. I looked sideways at her and she was sound asleep all spread out, which meant her foot crashed down on my stomach when she rolled over. I was still in my clothes from yesterday. I must have fallen asleep when Dad was reading and Mom and Dad didn't want to wake me.

I took Lauren's leg and lightly pushed her so she would roll over the other way.

Smack.

"Ooowwwww!" Lacey screeched.

I leaned up on my elbow and looked over across Lauren, and Lacey was still in bed. She must have fallen asleep too, because she was still in her clothes from yesterday.

"Oowww, Lauren get off me!" Lacey mumbled.

When I rolled Lauren over her arm went flying and she smacked Lacey right across her face.

Lauren slowly opened her eyes.

"Hey, what are you guys doing in my bed?" she asked confused.

"We all fell asleep during Dad's story," I said.

"Oh yeah," Lacey said sleepily.

"Hey guys, listen!" I announced.

"To what?" Lacey asked.

"Exactly!" I jumped up. "The storm is over!"

"We can go find Chloe!" Lacey yelled.

All three of us practically fell out of Lauren's bed and we ran down the hallway to Mom and Dad's room.

Empty.

We all turned around and went running down the stairs as fast as we could, and ran in the kitchen.

"Do I have little girls or a herd of elephants?" Dad asked as he and Mom were drinking their coffee.

"Let's go let's go let's go!" Lacey shouted. "Come on the rain has stopped!"

"Hold on," Dad said, "we're going."

"But now!" I pleaded.

"I wants to go too!" Lauren said. We were all shouting at once. We didn't even hear Mom's phone ringing.

"Calm down, be quiet, let me answer this," Mom announced and hit the speaker button on the phone.

"Hello?"

"Is this the Robbins household?" a lady asked.

"Yes," Mom almost shouted over the noise.

"I'm calling from the animal clinic," she said.

Everyone froze.

"Yes?" Mom continued.

The lady on the phone kept talking.

"This morning a woman brought in a little puppy she found yesterday afternoon, and we checked her for a microchip and your information came up. Are you missing a little puppy named Chloe?"

"YES!" We all shouted!

"Is she OK?" Mom asked.

"She's perfectly fine," the lady answered. "You can come pick her up anytime."

"We're on our way!" Dad answered.

He swooped Lauren up in his arms, opened the door and said, "Let's Go!"

We all ran out to the car and piled in. I never saw Dad start the car so fast!

Lacey sat there looking at me smiling and crying at the same time. I was doing the same. Someone found Chloe. Yesterday afternoon. That meant Chloe wasn't left out in the storm all night.

Dad pulled in front of the animal clinic and we all almost fell out of the car and ran for the door.

When we opened the clinic's door there was a lady behind the counter talking to a woman. And there was Chloe standing on the counter.

When Chloe saw us she yelped and started wagging her tail so fast I thought it was going to fall off!!

"CHLOE!" We all shouted and ran over to her. She was perfect! She even had a big pink bow around her neck. We put her on the floor and she kept running to me and Lauren and Lacey wagging her tail and climbing on us trying to lick us. Everyone was laughing.

"Thank you so much," Dad said to the woman.

"Oh you're welcome," she said. "I'm just sorry that I couldn't contact you last night. But when the storm was so bad and my power went out, I decided to wait until first thing this morning. I knew she had to belong to someone."

"Where did you find her?" Mom asked.

"I was on my way home from a meeting that I was at all day, and I remembered I hadn't checked my mail, so I decided to stop at the mailbox quickly and pick up my mail before the storm got any worse. I parked my car right in front of my community mailbox on Maple Street, and when I got out I saw this little puppy huddled underneath it. I knew she was lost, and there was no one around with it raining so hard, so I picked her up and put her in my car to keep her safe and get her out of the storm."

Chloe was rolling on her back still wagging her tail and trying to lick us. We were laughing so hard!

"We can't thank you enough!" Dad said.

"I'm just glad she had the microchip," she said.

"Oh and one other thing," the woman continued, "she was so wet and muddy when I got her home, I gave her a bath. She put up such a fuss, but I finally got her clean. I don't think she really likes baths."

Lacey and I just looked at each other and burst out laughing.

ABOUT THE AUTHOR

I am a mother of two daughters and a faithful student of the "Positive Thinking" philosophy, as well as a believer in the "Law of Attraction". Unfortunately, it was not until I was in my thirties that I was introduced to, and began to take part in, these teachings. Fascinated with these studies, there was one question I would ask myself every time I was introduced to a new author or book on this topic – why wasn't I taught this as a child? If I had been, I wouldn't have developed some of the unhealthy attitudes and opinions that I worked for years to reverse.

My series of books contains subtle messages of positive thinking, as well as a reminder to always have a "don't give up" attitude on a child's level. The messages are entwined in mysteries or short stories that are entertaining for the child to read themselves, or for someone to read aloud. I hope you and your children enjoy them. Thank you.

Lynn Marie Lusch

To read more stories about Lindsey, her family, friends, and pets, look for these books on Amazon.com:

Millie's Lost Adventure
Lauren's Angel
Lindsey and the Christmas Puppy
Millie Meets Bugger
Second Grade Spelling Challenge
Radar and the Time Capsule Mystery
A Puppy Fashion Show
Kitten Trouble
Maddie Moves Away
Lindsey Goes to the Dentist

Parents, please visit us on Facebook to stay up to date on new releases and other exciting news: www.facebook.com/lynnsgirls

Like our page and share your and your child's favorite part of the book!

Also visit our Blog: lynnsgirlsbooks.wordpress.com for musings from the author and exclusive information about future books!

Contact us at: lynnsgirlsbooks@gmail.com

Made in the USA
Columbia, SC
29 January 2018